MY DAD AT THE ZOO

Coralie Saudo
Kris Di Giacomo

DISCARD

ENCHANTED LION BOOKS
NEW YORK

Most of the time my dad is really great,
cuddly even, when he wants to be.
But Sunday mornings
usually start out like this:

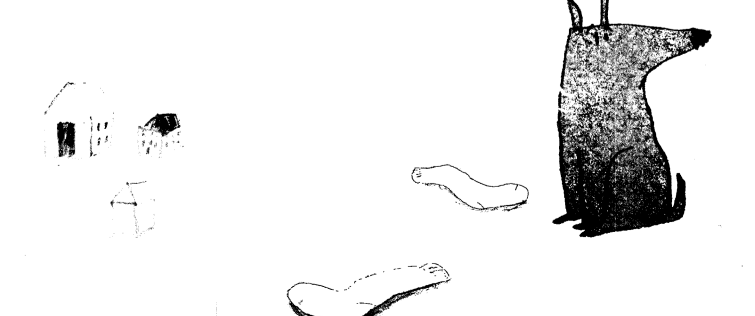

"everybody **UP!**

I **want** to go to the **ZOO!**"

I'm still sleepy...
But Dad doesn't care!
He throws me on his back
and does the galloping camel
all the way to the zoo.

I have to admit, it's pretty funny.

But standing in line for the tickets isn't funny at all.

Dad bounces around and squirms every which way.

And the longer we wait,
the more ideas he has about how
to cut the line
Like shouting,

Pee!

"I have to

Let me in!"

Once inside, the chase begins.

"Wait up, Dad!"

But Dad is way too busy
to pay any attention to me.

He's grimacing at the gorillas,
flirting with the flamingos,
pattering like the penguins,
terrorizing the turtles.

And then suddenly:

I don't see him any more!

Phew! I found him.
Where, you ask?
In front of the ice cream vendor, of course.

It's not snack time yet,
but it's clearly time
for a melt down!

"SON! I WANT an ice cream!"

I try to explain that it's still
too early for ice cream,
but Dad rolls around on the ground,
turning red with rage.

QUICK, I need a plan to distract him.

"Look, Dad!
A porcupine is escaping!
He's going that way!"

Success!
Dad forgets all about
the ice cream.

For two whole minutes we look
for my imaginary porcupine...

Then Dad spots his
favorite animal.

He tips his hat to say hello.

The elephant reaches out
and grabs it!

Dad cracks up, but not me.
That must be the eighth
hat he's lost at the zoo!

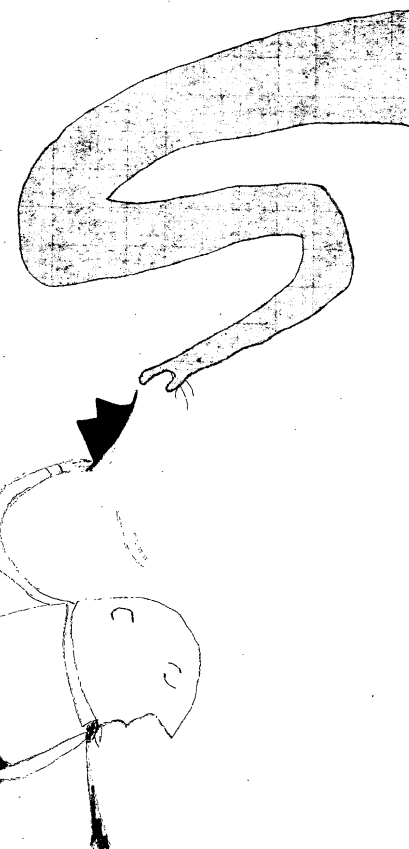

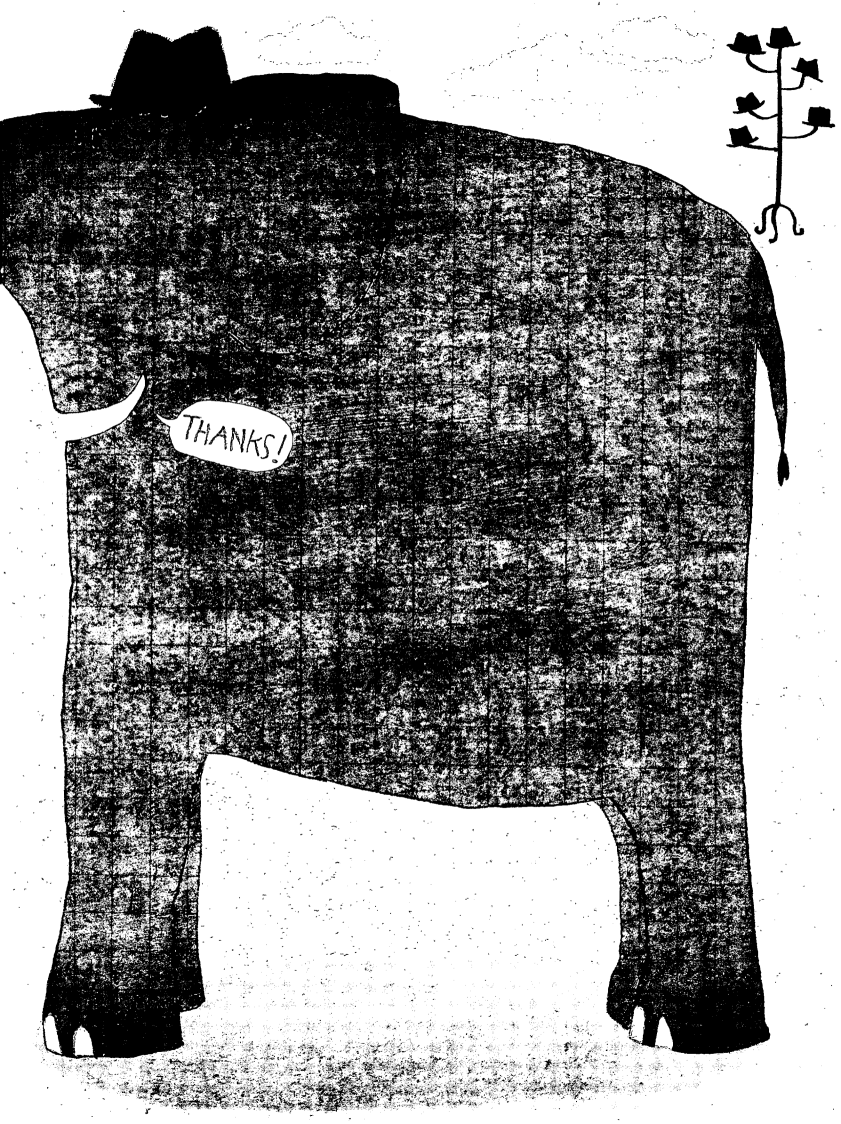

Next, we watch the sea lion show
and the piranha feeding.

What a day!

Finally, it's snack time.
We sit down but Dad can't keep still.

SPLAT!

There goes the ice cream.
Oh well, one more for the ants.

At last, it's time to say,

"goodbye"

to all the animals.

The chameleons,
the tapirs,
the parrots...

Dad doesn't want to miss anyone,
so we go through the entire zoo
one more time. I am exhausted!

But the worst is still to come:

THE SOUVENIR SHOP.

I hold Dad's hand with all my might,
trying to keep him from going in.
But Dad is still bigger and
stronger than me...

He makes a beeline for the
stuffed pigeons and screams

"IT'S
SOOO
CUTE!'"

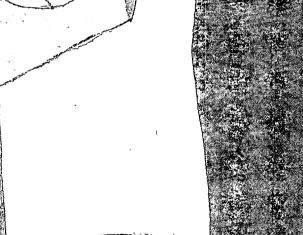

Dad starts to sulk.
The galloping camel
has turned into
a sluggish snail.

And me?
I'm wiped out.

It's true…my dad is really great.
And he's cuddly…really he is!

But Sundays at the zoo
are no picnic.

See ya,
Dad!

So the next time we come,
I think I'll just leave him here.

That'll teach him!